Animals in My Yard

Snakes

by Amy McDonald

BLASTOFF! Beginners

BELLWETHER MEDIA • MINNEAPOLIS, MN

Blastoff! Beginners are developed by literacy experts and educators to meet the needs of early readers. These engaging informational texts support young children as they begin reading about their world. Through simple language and high frequency words paired with crisp, colorful photos, Blastoff! Beginners launch young readers into the universe of independent reading.

Sight Words in This Book

and	in	some	what
can	is	the	with
do	little	their	
eat	long	they	
for	new	to	
have	not	too	

This edition first published in 2021 by Bellwether Media, Inc.

No part of this publication may be reproduced in whole or in part without written permission of the publisher. For information regarding permission, write to Bellwether Media, Inc., Attention: Permissions Department, 6012 Blue Circle Drive, Minnetonka, MN 55343.

Library of Congress Cataloging-in-Publication Data

Names: McDonald, Amy, author.
Title: Snakes / by Amy McDonald.
Description: Minneapolis, MN : Bellwether Media, 2021. | Series: Blastoff! beginners : Animals in my yard | Includes bibliographical references and index. | Audience: Ages PreK-2 | Audience: Grades K-1 |
Identifiers: LCCN 2020029480 (print) | LCCN 2020029481 (ebook) | ISBN 9781644873625 (library binding) | ISBN 9781648340635 (ebook)
Subjects: LCSH: Snakes--Juvenile literature.
Classification: LCC QL666.O6 M388 2021 (print) | LCC QL666.O6 (ebook) | DDC 597.96--dc23
LC record available at https://lccn.loc.gov/2020029480
LC ebook record available at https://lccn.loc.gov/2020029481

Text copyright © 2021 by Bellwether Media, Inc. BLASTOFF! BEGINNERS and associated logos are trademarks and/or registered trademarks of Bellwether Media, Inc.

Editor: Christina Leaf   Designer: Jeffrey Kollock

Printed in the United States of America, North Mankato, MN.

Table of Contents

Snakes!	4
Body Parts	6
The Lives of Snakes	12
Snake Facts	22
Glossary	23
To Learn More	24
Index	24

Snakes!

What is in the grassssss?
Hello, little snake!

Body Parts

Snakes have long bodies. They have **scales**.

scales

Snakes **shed** their skin.
New skin grows.

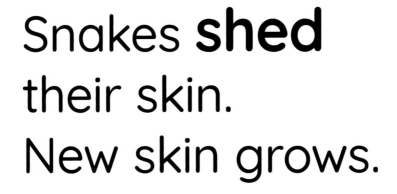

old skin

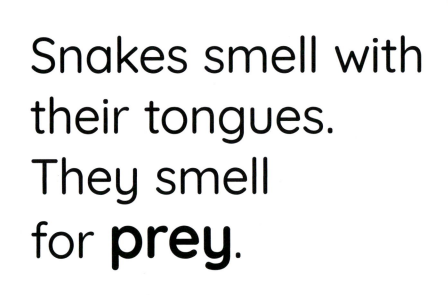

Snakes smell with their tongues. They smell for **prey**.

The Lives of Snakes

Snakes hunt for food. They eat frogs, mice, and birds.

frogs

Snakes do not chew. They eat animals whole.

Some animals eat snakes. Birds and foxes hunt snakes.

Snakes hide in the grass. They **slither** to move.

Snakes can swim, too. Swim away, snake!

Snake Facts

Snake Body Parts

long body

scales

tongue

Snake Food

frogs

mice

birds

Glossary

prey

animals that are food for other animals

scales

small, hard plates that cover an animal's body

shed

to lose or drop

slither

to slide across the ground

To Learn More

ON THE WEB

FACTSURFER

Factsurfer.com gives you a safe, fun way to find more information.

1. Go to www.factsurfer.com.

2. Enter "snakes" into the search box and click 🔍.

3. Select your book cover to see a list of related content.

Index

animals, 14, 16
birds, 12, 13, 16
bodies, 6
chew, 14
eat, 12, 14, 16
food, 12
foxes, 16
frogs, 12
grass, 4, 18

hide, 18
hunt, 12, 16
mice, 12, 13
move, 18
prey, 10, 13
scales, 6, 7
shed, 8
skin, 8
slither, 18

smell, 10
swim, 20
tongues, 10, 11

The images in this book are reproduced through the courtesy of: Eric Isselee, front cover, pp. 22, 23 (scales); fivespots, p. 3; PetlinDmitry, p. 4; teekaygee, pp. 4-5; Audrey Snider-Bell, pp. 6-7; Mara Fribus, p. 8; Joe Blossom/Alamy, pp. 8-9; Jason Patrick Ross, pp. 10-11; Gerry Bishop, pp. 12-13; Matt Jeppson, p. 12; jitkagold, p. 13 (mice); Gualberto Becerra, p. 13; Michell Gilders, pp. 14-15; Spark Dust, pp. 16-17; Christopher Unsworth, pp. 18-19; Jack Wood, pp. 20-21; Bradley van der Westhuizen/ Alamy, p. 22 (frogs); Alan Tunnicliffe/ Alamy, p. 22 (mice); Ancha Chiangmai, p. 22 (birds); Artem Onoprienko, p. 23 (prey); Wasan Ritthawon, p. 23 (shed); Jay Ondreicka, p. 23 (slither).